# Clementine

## and the Family Meeting

# Clementine
## and the Family Meeting

SARA PENNYPACKER

PICTURES BY
*Marla Frazee*

SCHOLASTIC INC.
New York  Toronto  London  Auckland
Sydney  Mexico City  New Delhi  Hong Kong

Many thanks to Claire Thompson for her drawing on page 9 and for her handwriting help on pages 52 and 53.

ISBN 978-0-545-39913-5

12 11 10 9 8 7 6 5 4 3 2 1     11 12 13 14 15 16/0

Printed in the U.S.A.                              23

First Scholastic printing, September 2011

This book is set in Fournier.

The illustrations for this book were done with pen and ink on Strathmore paper.

# Clementine
## and the Family Meeting

# CHAPTER

# I

The very first thing Margaret said when she sat down next to me on the bus Monday morning was that I looked terrible. "You have droopy eyebags and a pasty complexion. Absolutely no glow. What's the matter?"

"I'm having a nervous breakdown," I told her. "Our FAMILY MEETING! sign is up, and I have to wait until tonight to find out if I'm in trouble."

"Of course you're in trouble," Margaret said. "Probably something really big. Bright pink blush and a sparkly eye shadow is what I recommend."

This winter vacation, Margaret visited her father

in Hollywood, California. When she got back, I had to listen for three hundred hours to how great his new girlfriend was. "She's the makeup artist for his commercials," Margaret said all melty-voiced, as if *she* was the one who was in love with this Heather person.

"Someone who puts makeup on people isn't an artist," I informed Margaret. "My mother is an artist. Not her."

"Heather is too an artist," Margaret snorted. "And she's been teaching me some of her professional techniques." Then Margaret had blabbered on and on about advanced lip-gloss tips and the proper application of eyeliner until I thought I would die of bore-dumb.

Whenever Margaret talks about makeup, I feel exactly the way I felt when we took my grandparents to the airport so they could move to Florida: lonely. Even though Margaret isn't going anywhere, when she talks about makeup, I feel like I'm back at the airport again and she's getting on a plane for a long trip to somewhere without me.

"I don't need any blush!" I yelled, a little louder than I meant to. "I don't need any makeup at all! I just need to know what I'm in trouble about!"

Margaret rolled her eyes at me and then dug around in her pocketbook. She pulled out a pointy silver tube that looked dangerous, like a bullet.

"Margaret!" I gasped. "Are you putting on lipstick?"

Margaret smeared the lipstick on, pooched her lips out, and smucked them at me. "Yep," she said. *Smuck-smuck-smuck.* "So what? I'll take it off before we get there."

"*Mar! Ga! Ret!*" I cried. "You are *ten! Years! Old!*"

Margaret had had her tenth birthday while she was on that Hollywood vacation. Since then, she'd been acting like she was twenty-five or something. Sometimes I didn't even recognize her. Plus, I didn't get to go to a party for her.

Margaret smucked her shiny pink lips at me again. "Heather says I am very mature for my age." She waved the lipstick tube in front of my face. "You want some?"

I tapped my lips. "Mouth germs," I warned her. "I can feel them crawling around."

Margaret yanked the lipstick back in horror. She spent the rest of the bus ride wiping everything in her pocketbook with hand sanitizer. Being a germ-maniac was about the only thing I recognized about the new Margaret.

I opened my backpack and pulled out my

IMPORTANT PAPERS folder and found a good surprise: the science fair project report Waylon and I had written was still in there! I'm supposed to keep it until the end of the project, and every day that it's still in my backpack feels like a miracle.

As I started reading over the report, I calmed down. This is because lately I really like science class.

I didn't always. In the beginning, science class was a big disappointment, let me tell you.

On the first day of third grade, Mrs. Resnick, the science teacher, had started talking about what a great year it was going to be.

I looked around the science room.

No monkeys with funnel hats and electrodes. No alien pods leaking green slime. No human heads sitting on platters under glass jars talking to each other, like I'd seen in a movie once, and don't bother telling my parents about it because I was grounded for a week already and so was Uncle Frank, who brought me to the movie.

No smoking test tubes, no sizzling magnetic rays, no rocket launch controls. Just some posters on the walls and a bunch of tall tables with sinks, as if all you would do in a room like this was wash your hands. Margaret had told me she liked science class, and now I knew why: Margaret says "Let's go wash our hands" the way other people say "Let's go to a party and eat cake!"

"Does anyone have any questions?" Mrs. Resnick had asked that first day.

I sure did. I wanted to ask, "You call this a science room?" But instead, I just said, "Excuse me, I think there's been a mistake," in my most polite voice.

"A mistake?" Mrs. Resnick asked.

"Right," I said. "I'm in the wrong science room."

"The wrong science room?" she repeated.

8

I nodded. "I want the one with the invisibility chamber and mind-control buttons and mutant brains spattered on the ceiling. The one with the experiments."

"I want that one, too," Waylon said. I gave him a big smile.

"Oh, there are plenty of experiments going on here," Mrs. Resnick said. "We're going to have quite a year."

Mrs. Resnick seemed nice, so I didn't tell her the other bad news: that she had the wrong hair. Scientists are supposed to have wild science-y hair— here is a picture of that: But hers was just kind of normal supermarket-y, television-mother-y kind of hair. Probably she was embarrassed about that.

Now, though, I like science class. Mrs. Resnick is a good teacher, even with her normal hair. I like our science fair project, and I like our rat, Eighteen. I like that I got Waylon for a partner. All the kids begged him to be their partner, because he's the scienciest kid in third grade. But he picked me, because I'm the only one who believes he's going to be a superhero when he grows up.

And today, I had an extra thing to like about science class: for forty whole minutes, I wouldn't have to think about our family meeting or Margaret's lipstick smucking.

"We're here," I said. "Wipe your mouth off, Margaret."

Margaret scowled, but she wiped off the lipstick and we went into school.

It was an extra-boring day, but finally it was time to line up to go to the science room. As soon as we got there, I saw that something was wrong. I ran over to the rats' cages. "Eighteen's missing!" I cried.

I shook the trail mix we used as treats and called for him, while Waylon poked through the sawdust. "He's really missing, all right," Waylon announced.

Mrs. Resnick came over and frowned into the cage. "They were all here Friday when I left. Check through the bedding again—I'll bet he's just hiding."

I feathered away the wood curls more carefully.

And then I saw. "Look," I said. In the back corner, under the water bottle, a rat-belly-size hole had been chewed through the plastic floor.

Mrs. Resnick was really frowning now. "He's probably been gone all weekend. Still, let's search the room."

We looked everywhere. We looked in the second graders' volcano models. We plowed through the trays of seeds the fourth graders were germinating. We poked through the fifth graders' crystal collections. We even looked in the paper-towel dispenser.

No Eighteen.

After a while, the other kids had to go back to

their rat-training, and only Waylon and I kept looking. When the bell rang, we still hadn't found him.

"Maybe he'll show up when I feed the other rats this afternoon," Mrs. Resnick said. "You two head back to your class now." Waylon and I said all right and went back to 3B. But it wasn't all right.

A little while ago, my kitten, Moisturizer, got lost in Boston. All the bad feelings I had when he was missing—worrying about him being scared,

or getting hurt, and about whether it was my fault—came back over me.

All day long, I worried about that little rat. I had to hear about a hundred "Clementine, pay attention!"s from my teacher, and every time, I *was* paying attention.

I was paying attention to Maria's chunky boots that looked like tires on the bottom, and worrying about someone stomping on Eighteen. I was paying attention out the window to all that ice and snow and imagining how cold Eighteen would be if he'd gotten outside. When the janitor came down the hall, I was paying attention to his gigantic vacuum cleaner and thinking how he wouldn't even notice if a little tiny white rat got sucked up inside. After that, I started wondering if our school had a trash compactor, and that got me so worried I almost gave myself a heart attack.

Finally, after three hundred hours, the school's-over bell rang. I got my stuff from the coatrack and asked Mr. D'Matz if I could go back to the science room.

He pointed to the clock. "Don't miss the bus."

The bell rings at two fifteen and the buses open their doors at two twenty and my bus is the second to leave, which is at two twenty-eight, so I had thirteen minutes. "I won't," I said. I set my inside clock for twelve minutes, because one had already been wasted talking to my teacher. My inside clock keeps perfect time, and so I am never late for anything. Okay, fine, I'm late a lot, but it's only because I forget to *set* my inside clock. But I was remembering now.

I ran down the hall even though the rule is no running in the hall, and I was there in fifty-one seconds.

I dumped my coat and stuff on top of the bookshelf and skidded over to the cage. "He didn't
come back?" I asked.

"Who?" Mrs. Resnick asked back.

"Our rat, who's missing," I reminded her in a patient, kind voice, the voice I wish people would use with me if I forget something. "Didn't he come back when you fed them?"

She said, "No, sorry."

I sprinkled some trail mix outside his cage in case he came back, and then my inside clock said it was time to go. On the bus, I worried about Eighteen so much my head hurt.

# CHAPTER 2

Usually when I get home, things get better, but not that day.

"Hi, honey," my mom said when I came in the door. "Where's your hat?"

"My hat?" I felt on top of my head. "My hat!"

I *love* my hat! My grandmother knit it out of my favorite colors, which are all of them, and sent it to me on my birthday. When I put it on, I could almost feel her soft hands on my head.

"Where is my hat?" I wailed. "I know I had it when I was leaving. . . ."

"Well then, it's either at school or on the bus. Remember to get it tomorrow. You must be freezing, though. How about if we fix some hot chocolate?"

When I went over to the refrigerator to get the milk out, I saw our FAMILY MEETING! sign again. A worried feeling spread into exactly the place that had opened up for the hot chocolate. I pointed to the sign.

"What's on the agenda?" I asked. Agenda is Latin for "list of stuff to talk about," so when you say it, you're saving your mouth a lot of work. Plus, you sound smart.

My mom took the jug from me and sniffed it, and then nodded at it with her *Good-job!* smile, as if she was proud of our milk for not turning sour. She looked back at me. "What? Oh, the agenda?" She poured some milk into a saucepan on the stove. "You'll find out tonight. Your brother's asleep on the couch. Would you go wake him, please?"

I said, "Sure!" with a giant smile, in case what was on the agenda was *Help out more cheerfully.* As I went by, I picked my wet mittens off the floor and hung them over the radiator, in case it was *Don't be messy with your winter clothes.* And when I woke Acorn Squash, I sat down and said hello to his feet along with him, loud enough for my mom to hear, in case it was *Be more patient with your brother.*

My mom set three mugs and a bowl of almonds on the kitchen table, and we all sat at our places. Right away, my brother started to tell us about going sledding with Mitchell on Sunday, which is a story we have heard three hundred times already.

"What do we have to talk about tonight?" I tried again, when he took a break. Then I said, "Please-pass-the-almonds-excuse-me-thank-you," in case it was *Better table manners.*

"The meeting's *tonight*," my mother said. "You'll have to wait until then to find out."

I heaved such a deep sigh into my mug that my hot chocolate sloshed. Waiting is my hardest thing.

Especially for family meetings.

Because even though my parents say they are

about things we have to talk over as a family, I have noticed they are usually about something I am doing wrong.

If my father calls a meeting, it's usually about his tools—about how he needs to know where they are because of his work, and so it's important to put them back when you borrow them. Even though it's a *family* meeting, he looks right at me when he's explaining this. Then he says, "Oh, never mind. I forgot that I let your uncle Frank use those vise grips last week. Sorry, Clementine."

Okay, fine, it only happened that way once.

The other times I get up and dig around under my bed until I find the tool my father must have dropped when he leaned over to say good night to me the night before.

When my mother calls a family meeting, it's usually because she thinks my brother and I are eating too much junk food. She talks about nutrition for a while and says we have to feed our bodies well. And my father says, "Right! If I had a Rolls-Royce, I sure wouldn't put cheap gas in the tank!"

Turnip and I feel so good about being the Rolls-Royces of kids that we get up and pretend to throw away our gum. While we're up we check on the candy we keep hidden in the Play-Doh box, and then we come back and say we feel a lot healthier now, thanks, and for the rest of the meeting, Squash pretends he's a car.

No matter who calls the meeting, I make sure to remind everybody of what a great idea it would be if our family got a gorilla. That's *my* agenda.

I looked around the table. My mother and my brother were just sitting there drinking hot chocolate, crunching almonds, and laughing as if the

FAMILY MEETING! sign was still back in the junk drawer where it belonged. The worried feeling crawled through my whole body like worms.

"So," I said, "has Uncle Frank borrowed any of Dad's tools lately?"

"Not that I know of," Mom said.

I wiped off my cocoa mustache with a napkin and took some more almonds from the bowl. "We sure are eating healthy these days."

"We're doing pretty well," Mom agreed. Then she collected our empty mugs, as if that was the end of that.

My brother went off to play in the living room, and I slumped over onto the table.

"What's the matter?" my mom asked, patting my back.

"Everything," I sighed. "First, Eighteen is missing."

"Eighteen?"

My nervous breakdown had made my mouth too tired to talk, so I pulled out my science project report and handed it over.

My mother read it out loud.

Our class is testing different things that might make a rat learn better. They are called factors. Each team chose a different factor to test.

For example, Lilly and Maria are playing music for their rat while it practices the maze. Willy and Norris-Boris-Morris put a television show on. That's not such a hot idea because Willy and Norris-Boris end up watching the show instead of their rat. Plus, lots of times the show is about things that might scare a rat, like cats—there sure are a lot of cats on television.

Waylon and Clementine decided to find out if eating snacks would help a rat learn. Because we both think that eating snacks helps us when we're trying to learn things.

Eighteen's doing great learning the maze. The only problem is that with so many treats he's getting kind of fat— it's hard for him to squeeze through some of the tunnels. At the end, we will test all the rats against each other, and then we'll know.

"What a wonderful report!" my mother said.

I tried to lift my head from the table, but it was too tired. "Waylon wrote it," I admitted. "I only did the part about Willy and Norris-Boris."

"Well, it sounds like a good project," she said.

"Not without a rat, it won't be."

Just then, my father walked in. And suddenly, my nervous breakdown was over!

"Oh, wow!" I said, jumping up. My father was wearing his new tool belt. It was the most beautiful thing I'd ever seen in my whole entire life. It was rugged looking but made of soft, bendy leather, the color of butterscotch pudding, and covered with loops and rings and hooks and snaps. It looked like a holster for a cowboy with lots of guns.

"Can I try it on? Please?"

My father poured himself a mug of hot chocolate and shook his head sadly, as though he was thinking of the most tragic tragedy in the world. "Sorry, Sport. This tool belt was handed down through fourteen generations of the men in my family. It's a priceless heirloom."

Mostly I think my dad's jokes are funny. Sometimes, though, they are N-O-T, *not*.

"Dad. We got it yesterday at Hardware Depot."

"Oh, right," my dad said. He drank some cocoa and then complained about how much work he

had to do. "My beeper's been going crazy all afternoon. Winter! The boiler's thumping, the pump's off on the seventh floor, and Mrs. Jacobi's windows are iced shut. I'll be lucky if I'm back for dinner."

"Don't forget the meeting tonight," my mom said.

I slumped back down to my chair. "Just tell me what I did wrong," I sighed. "Say what the meeting's about, and I'll promise to do better."

My mother sat down next to me. "Oh, honey, you didn't do anything wrong. Nothing at all. Is that what you've been thinking? No, the meeting's for . . . something else."

I lifted my head and *Really?*-eyed her.

"Really." She smiled.

My dad was smiling, too.

"I'm not in trouble?" I asked them. "And the meeting's not about a problem?"

"Nope," my dad said. "The meeting's about a good thing, in fact. A good surprise. Something we've been waiting for, for a long time."

I felt so relieved, I decided to try again. "Then, could I try your tool belt on when you get back?"

"Not a chance. When I get back, I'm going to have to lock it in the safe," my dad said. "You see, this tool belt is a priceless treasure from the Ming dynasty. It's irreplaceable. If anything happened to it—"

"Dad," I said. "It came from Hardware Depot. You could just buy another."

"Oh, right," he said. But then he went off to see about Mrs. Jacobi's frozen windows, muttering about winter.

One way that I am like my fruit name is that I have lots of sections. Right now, a couple of Clementine sections were worrying about Eighteen. A few Clementine sections were thinking about that tool belt, about how great it would be to try it on. A few of them were mad at my dad for thinking it was funny not to share it. But most of my sections were so happy to find out that I wasn't in trouble!

My mother went into the living room to work on some drawings. My brother watched a video about bulldozers. And all afternoon, I tried to guess what the good surprise was.

Finally, finally, it was after dinner. We cleaned the table—which took a while because when we weren't looking, Spinach had hidden his little toy trucks in the ziti—and sat back down in our family-meeting places. Our family-meeting places are the same as our regular places, except that my brother has figured out that whatever the meeting is about, he and I are on the same team, so he sits on my lap. This gives me hope for him.

Moisturizer jumped onto my lap too, and then my dad called the meeting to order.

"We are a very lucky family," he said. "Very lucky."

"What's on the agenda?" I asked.

"I'm getting to that," my dad said. "Now, families change. They grow. It's hard to believe, but you're eight and a half now, and your brother's almost four."

I clapped my hands over my brother's ears. "Should we have a surprise party for him? You know what would make a great present? A gorilla!"

"His birthday's not for a few months," my mom said. "I vote we table that discussion for another time."

"Well, so what's the good thing we have to talk about tonight?" I asked.

My dad looked at my mom and raised his eyebrows. My mom looked back at him and smiled. She waved her palm at him like a game-show host, as if to say, "Show us these great prizes, Bill!"

My dad looked at my mom again, and this time he looked like he was going to cry! Not in a sad way, but in an "I can't believe how lucky I am that you're here" way. Which was nuts, because my mom is *always* here.

"Families grow," he said again. "And tonight..."
He stopped and smiled at my mom again. "Tonight,
your mother and I want to talk to you about . . .
an addition to our family. Our family is about to
grow again."

And then finally I figured out what he was
saying! I slid Pea Pod off my lap and jumped up
to give my dad and mom a hug.

"Yes! Thank you! Yes! You won't be sorry, I promise I'll take good care of it, you'll barely even notice it's here . . . Thank you!"

Cauliflower was sitting on the floor, looking between me and our parents, completely clueless. I leaned over and squeezed him hard. "We're getting a gorilla, after all!"

My mom fell back against her chair, laughing. "Oh, Clementine," she said. "It's definitely not a gorilla!"

I was a little tiny bit relieved. The truth is, since I got my kitten, I'm not sure I really want a gorilla anymore. That would be a really big litter box.

I studied my parents. "What is it, then? A pony? We're getting a *pony*?"

My dad pulled me over to him and held my hands. "We're talking about a new baby. A brother or a sister for you two. What do you think about that?"

CHAPTER

3

What I thought about that was N-O, *no thanks!*

I yelled it.

"No thanks!" Parsnip echoed. Then he looked up at me. "No thanks what?"

"No thanks to more people! Our family is four. There are four sides to a puzzle so we can all work on it at once. Hot dogs come in packages of eight, so we can each have two. At the playground, four is an even number for the seesaws. Four can all be together in the car. Four can be two and two sometimes, and nobody is lonely. Two kids and two grown-ups. Two boys and two girls. There are four sides to the kitchen table, so we each get one. Four is a perfect number for a family!"

While I'd been explaining all this, my brother had snuck over to his favorite cupboard and thrown all the pots and pans out, like a personal-size tornado. He was sitting inside now, crashing lids together.

I pointed to the mess in the kitchen. "Look at us! Lima Bean puts toy trucks in the ziti and we used a drill gun to stir the muffins this morning because we couldn't find the mixer and my rat is missing, which isn't my fault, and so is my hat, and maybe that *is* my fault, but how is a baby going to help with anything, that's what I want to know! It's all moving too fast and we're not ready."

"Oh, honey," my mom said. "Life is *always* moving too fast and we're *never* ready. That's how life *is*. But somehow that's just perfect." She dragged Zucchini out of the cupboard and hauled him off to get his pajamas on.

"Your mother," my dad said, "is exactly right. Things are always changing—that's life. And this?" He spread his hands to the tornadoed kitchen. "Us? Toy-truck ziti, missing hats, drill-gun mixers? Well, this is how we roll, Clementine. This is how we roll."

He started picking up the pots and pans, and after a while, I went over and helped him.

I didn't say, "What if we didn't roll for a little while? What if we just stood still?" even though my mouth was nearly bursting with the words. But I guess my dad could see me thinking it any way. When the kitchen was picked up, he hoisted himself onto the counter and pushed back the cutting board so I could climb up beside him. "Do you remember how you felt when Gram and Pop moved to Florida?" he asked.

I nodded.

"You thought you'd never see them again, and you were upset because you liked having them live just a couple of blocks away. And how did that work out?"

"Part good and part bad," I answered. "I can't see them when I want to, and I miss them. But now I have someone to write letters to, and I like that. And they come here in the summer and stay for a whole week, and I get to sleep on the couch. And then in the winter we go there for a week, and I get to call out 'Lucky legs eleven!' at bingo and drive the golf cart for Pop, and a lemon fell out of a tree right onto my head, and in two years—Disney World. So, part good and part bad."

"That's what most change is—part good and part bad," my dad said. "Right?" he asked my mom, who had just come back with my brother.

My mom ignored him. "Did I hear something about driving a golf cart? And what's this about bingo?"

My father laughed. "Our daughter has a secret life in Florida, apparently. Part good and part bad for us, too. Anyway, I think it's up to us which part to concentrate on. That's what makes the difference."

I jumped down from the counter. "I want to write Gram and Pop a letter right now," I said. "Do they know yet?"

"No," my mom said. "We wanted to tell you two first. But we were planning on calling them tonight. In fact, let's get your brother to bed, and then we can call."

My mom asked my brother who should read his bedtime story to him, and for the first time ever, he picked . . . me!

"Really? Not Mom or Dad?"

Bean Sprout said yes again, and then he dragged me into his room. He lined all his trucks on the bed to get ready and he pulled a book from under his pillow.

Let me tell you, it was not much of a story—a bunch of trucks live together and crash into each other. That's all, and I'm not even kidding. But my brother loved it. As I read, he crashed his trucks together two by two and then tucked them under the covers to go to sleep.

When I was finished, he thanked me!

"You're welcome," I said, surprised. And then I looked at him—really looked at him. Usually

he looks like a puppy to me—little and round and always wiggling. But tonight, stretched out long in his big-boy bed with one of Mitchell's old baseball caps on, he looked like . . . a boy.

Which meant our family didn't have a baby in it anymore.

My dad held the phone up when I came into the living room. "Would you like to tell them, Clementine?" he asked.

I shook my head. "You do it."

I flopped onto the couch and listened. My mom sat down beside me and wrapped my curls around her fingers.

"It's wonderful . . . Yes, yes . . . July . . . wonderful," my dad was saying. "She feels fine . . . yes, it's wonderful . . ." And then he said "it's wonderful" a hundred more times.

Finally my dad handed the phone to me.

"Hi," I said. And then nothing else came out. Especially not "It's wonderful."

"So you're going to be a big sister again," my grandmother's voice said.

"I guess," I said.

"Well, I'd say this new baby is very lucky," Gram said. "You are an excellent big sister. Luckily, you don't take after your father at all in that respect."

I sat up. "What do you mean?"

"Well!" my grandmother said, and I could tell I was in for a long, juicy story. I suddenly wished Florida wasn't two thousand miles away, so I could sit beside her while she told it. "Well," she said again, "your father was four years old when Frank was born."

"Just like me," I interrupted. "I was four when Spinach was born."

"Well, that's right. But your father was a very different kind of four-year-old than you were. He was a hellion, that boy. He was practically feral. Your father, Clementine, was a four-year-old *maniac*. You, on the other hand, have always shown immensely good sense."

That was the first time in my entire life I'd ever heard anyone say I showed good sense. "Would you say that again, Gram?" I asked. "Really loud. I'm going to put you on speakerphone now."

"I'd be happy to, dear," my grandmother said. "You always showed such good sense around your little brother. Right from the beginning, you were very careful with him, very protective of him."

"I was? I don't remember that."

"Oh, yes," my grandmother said. "You were a wonderful big sister. Not like your father at all."

"Why? What did he do?" I looked over at my father. He made an innocent face and threw his hands up.

"Gracious, what didn't he do?" My grandmother's laughter filled our apartment. "We didn't think your Uncle Frank would live to see his first birthday. Your father was absolutely intent on

getting rid of him, from the day we brought him home from the hospital. I couldn't turn my back for a second. One time he filled up the baby carriage with pinecones."

"So you couldn't put Uncle Frank in it?"

"Oh, no, honey. Uncle Frank was already *in* the baby carriage," my grandmother said. "We had to dig him *out*."

"Now wait a minute," my dad began.

But my grandmother was just getting warmed up. "Another time, I found him trying to put the baby in the dryer. He said his diaper was wet. Thank goodness I got there before he figured out how to turn it on."

My father shook his head with a sad face. *She's a little crazy*, he mouthed. *It's all that Florida sun.*

My mother bent over the counter, scribbling something.

"And then there was the time with the garden

hose," my grandmother said. "Now, that was really—"

My dad sprang over and grabbed the phone and stabbed off the speaker button. "Well, now, I'm sure we don't need to go filling her head with any more stories," he said to my grandmother. "How's the weather down there these days?"

My mother tugged on my father's sleeve and held up her pad of paper. LUCKY LEGS ELEVEN!!! DRIVING THE GOLF CART!!! she'd scribbled in big capital letters, with about three hundred exclamation marks all around the page.

My father signaled *Later* to my mother, then said into the phone, "Well, we've had a big day here, lots of excitement. I think we'd better say good night now. Love to you and Pop." And he hung up before anybody could get into any more trouble.

I headed into my room and took out a notebook.

Dear Gram and Pop,

How are you I am fine. Well, not SO fine. I am still looking for the good part about a new baby. Could you tell more about what a good sister I was? About how I was so protective and showed immensely good sense? You can write on the back of this letter and also I will send some more paper so you can write a lot.

Love,
your granddaughter
(THE ONLY ONE YOU HAVE!)
(FOR NOW!!!)
Clementine

P. S. also I lost your hat and I am very sorry.

P. P. S. but I will find it!!!!!!!!!!!

P. P. P. S. Have you caught Mrs. Grocki cheating at bingo yet?

# CHAPTER
## 4

I told Margaret about the new baby on the bus ride Tuesday morning. She smoothed away some imaginary skirt wrinkles and then said, "That's going to ruin everything. I don't know why you're allowing it."

"What do you mean *allowing* it? What can I do?"

"Well, *I'd* move out," Margaret said, without even thinking about it for a second.

I tried to imagine Margaret not living in her looks-like-a-magazine-picture apartment, but I couldn't do it. "Where would you go? Hey, would you move in with me?"

Margaret gave me her "Are you crazy?" look. "I want my own room. You're out of rooms. I'd go live with my father."

"In California?"

Margaret nodded hard. "I'd have my own room there. With my own orange tree."

"You'd have an *orange tree*?"

"Yes. Right outside my bedroom window. So I could just reach out and pick oranges and eat them in bed."

Margaret was surprising me so much today, I was starting not to be surprised when she surprised me. Still. "Margaret . . . oranges, in *bed*? What about . . . ?"

"I'd keep a roll of paper towels beside the bed, of course," she said, as if she'd already planned out this California bedroom of hers. "And rubber gloves. And a wastepaper basket."

"Oh," I said. "Well, what about Mitchell?"

Margaret gave me another "Are you crazy?" look—high power this time. "He'd stay *here*. He could watch the baby when my mother goes to work. He'd have to change all the diapers. Ha!" Margaret stopped to shudder from the horror she'd be escaping.

Sometimes Margaret can get kind of carried away with an idea. "Your mother's not having a baby," I reminded her. "Mine is."

"I know," Margaret said. "I'm just saying *if.*"


At lunch, Waylon brought his tray over and sat down to give me some bad news. "If we don't find Eighteen, we'll have to do a different science project," he said.

Just hearing Waylon say we might not find him made my throat hurt. "I hadn't thought about that. What would we do instead?"

Waylon piled his carrot sticks onto his slice of pizza. "Vikings. Boarding their ship," he said.

I forgot that before Waylon eats something, it has to be in a battle. I waited and tried to think of what would make a good project. Maybe we could build a solar system. Maybe we could re-create the stomach of a *Tyrannosaurus rex*, with mashed-up triceratops guts and stuff.

Waylon scrambled his salad around the pizza. "Bad storm," he explained. Then he plowed his milk carton through the salad and crashed it into the Viking pizza-ship. Some of the carrot sticks fell into the water, and Waylon said they were dead immediately. He scooped up a bunch of the not-dead ones and started to whack the milk carton with them.

He glugged all the milk down. "Okay, Vikings win," he said. Then he took a bite of the ship.

"So what should we do?" I asked again. "If . . ."

"I think it should be about my superpowers," he said.

"Huh?"

"I think our project should be about my super-powers," Waylon repeated. He eyed my chicken drumlets for possible battle opportunities.

I pulled my tray closer. "It has to be something science-y, Waylon," I reminded him.

"Oh, my superpowers are science-y," Waylon said. "I'm going to be a very science-y superhero."

"Like what?" I asked.

"Like molecular transmogrification."

I started to get interested. Those were science-y words, all right. "What does that mean? Transmogrifi-whatever."

"It means I can walk through walls," Waylon said. "Or I'm starting to. I'm starting to be able to transmogrify the molecules of me through the molecules of the wall."

I got really excited—this was going to be way better than rats in a maze. It was even better than dinosaur guts! "You can really do that?"

"Sure. Watch." Waylon got up and walked up next to the NUTRITION ROCKS! poster. He pressed himself against the cinder-block wall so hard,

I thought his whole front would be one giant bruise.

"See?" he asked, through his smushed-up mouth. "I'm halfway through."

I was just about to laugh at his joke about squashing himself into the wall when he pulled away and turned to face me. His face was glowing, and I realized something: he believed it. He really believed he was transmogrifying his Waylon-molecules through the cafeteria wall.

"Um," I said. "But it has to be a project about testing factors, with control subjects . . . I think."

"That's where you come in," Waylon said. "You could be the control subject. Like rats One through Ten. You'll be the one who can't trans-mogrify, who proves that I can."

"Waylon, I don't think this is going to work," I said.

"Why not?" Waylon sat down again and

squint-eyed me. "Can you transmogrify too? Maybe we should use one of my other powers. . . ."

Just then the meanest lunchroom lady, the one who always says no to more chocolate milk, came out and glared at my class, which meant they were making the really big mistake of laughing when they were supposed to be eating.

I suddenly worried about Eighteen. I hoped he wouldn't wander into the lunchroom and think it was a good place to set up his new home. I never liked the story of the three blind mice, with all those carving knives.

When I turned back to Waylon, he was still going on about his superpowers,

and that made me feel really lonely, the way I did
when Margaret was blabbering about makeup. It
felt like now Waylon was getting on an airplane,
too, going somewhere I couldn't go. I finished
my lunch without talking anymore, and even the
applesauce tasted sour.

Waylon followed me out at recess and started in
again. Apparently, one of his superpowers wasn't
being able to figure out when people didn't want
to talk to him.

"Or maybe our project could be about my selec-
tive invisibility," he said.

"Invisibility?" I asked, getting a little bit
interested again.

"Uh-huh," Waylon said. "That's in develop-
ment, too. Haven't you ever noticed me getting
invisible? Sometimes it happens in gym class. I
don't like gym class."

"You get invisible in gym class?"

"Well, not yet," Waylon said. "I get kind of *cloudy*. You never noticed that?"

"No, sorry. How about we do something about dinosaurs? You can't get more science-y than dinosaurs."

"No, my superpowers are better. I'll show you my invisibility." Waylon looked around to make sure nobody was watching us. Then he rolled up his coat sleeve and his shirtsleeve and stuck out his arm. He squeezed his eyes shut and shook a little. "There," he said. "See?"

"See what?"

"My arm! See how it's a little bit invisible? How you can sort of see through it?"

"I see that you're shivering," I said. "It's freezing out."

"No, I'm getting invisible. Can't you see that?"

I looked at Waylon's face to see if he was kidding. He wasn't kidding.

"I don't know. Maybe a little. I have to go in now," I said. Because suddenly I did.

I ran across the playground and barged into our classroom, even though the rule is no coming back inside unless it's an emergency.

"It's an emergency," I said to Mr. D'Matz, who was correcting papers at his desk. "It's unfair our rat got lost, and it's unfair I have to do a whole new report, and it's unfair I have to have Waylon for a partner."

Mr. D'Matz leaned back in his chair. "I'm hearing the word *unfair* a lot, Clementine."

"That's because the whole thing is so unfair!" I said. "You might as well call it the Science *Un*-Fair project!"

"What exactly is so unfair?"

"Everything!"

"Everything?"

I nodded.

"Everything?"

"Well . . ."

"What is the biggest unfair thing about it?"

"That nobody asked us. They just decided."

"We've talked about this. It's the teacher's job to teach and the students' job to learn. Both of you have to decide about how best to do that."

"But what if we don't need another brother or sister? What if our family is perfect the way we are?"

I clapped my hands over my mouth when I realized what I had said. But Mr. D'Matz didn't seem surprised that we weren't talking about science fairs anymore. He just looked at me for a long while, and then he said, "Oh."

"Right," I said. "Oh. My parents should have asked my brother and me."

"Well, I think that's not how it usually goes. Parents decide these things."

"But they didn't tell us."

Mr. D'Matz nodded. "Parents often don't. Not for a while. They choose their timing."

I suddenly felt like I was going to cry if I said one more word, so I made my mouth into a ruler line.

Mr. D'Matz tipped his head. He looked as if he was trying to decide something. "You know, Clementine," he said after a while, "this is something we have in common."

I was so surprised I forgot about not talking. "Really? Your parents are having another baby, too?"

He laughed. "No. Well, at least I don't think so. . . . No, no, I'm sure they're not. What I meant was that my wife and I are expecting a baby. In just a few months."

"*What?*" Some of my Clementine sections were so excited! Mr. D'Matz was always bringing things in from home—his collection of Hawaiian shirts, his baseball cards. Zippy and Bump, the hamsters, were actually his. Maybe he'd bring his baby in, too, and pass it around.

But some of my sections were mad, too. "How come you didn't tell us?" I asked.

"Well, like I said, when to tell and who to tell—it's a private decision. For the parents."

"But that's not fair! You know stuff about us!"

My teacher pointed to a sign we'd put up at the beginning of school.

FAIR DOESN'T MEAN EVERYONE GETS THE SAME THING. FAIR MEANS EVERYONE GETS WHAT THEY NEED.

"Do you remember how that works?" he asked.

"I know," I said. "It means I get to stand up and wiggle around if I need to. It means Kyla gets to drink some orange juice when it's not even snack time."

"That's exactly right. And knowing what's going on in your lives helps me teach you."

"Well . . . don't you think it would help us to *learn* if we knew what was going on in *your* life?"

Mr. D'Matz was quiet for a minute as he thought about it. "You know, Clementine," he said at last, "you just might have a point. I'm going to have to think about it, though. For now, I'd appreciate it if you kept what I told you . . ." He made his fingers into the letter *P*, which is our secret signal.

"Got it," I said. "Private. Me, too. I'd appreciate it if you kept what I told you about my family"—I made the secret signal, too—"private."

Mr. D'Matz shook my hand, and then I went

back out to recess. I was surprised I didn't have to
duck when I went through the door, because I was
sure I had grown about three feet taller.

That afternoon, when the two-fifteen bell rang,
I hurried to the science room again, because one
good thing had happened during the day: I had
remembered where my hat was. I had thought
really hard about it, and suddenly I saw it like a

picture in my brain, tossed on the bookshelf in the science room yesterday afternoon. This means I have developed a photographic memory, which is really good news if I ever get on a game show—I am going to win every prize they have.

"I have to pull out the bookshelf," I told Mrs. Resnick as I skidded in. "I left my hat here yesterday, and it must have fallen down behind."

Mrs. Resnick helped me slide the bookshelf away from the wall. No hat. Just an empty floor.

"But it was there! I know it was!" I said. But okay, fine, now maybe I wasn't so sure.

"Well, hats don't get up and walk away by themselves. . . ." Mrs. Resnick said.

Which I knew. And which reminded me . . .

"He didn't come back, did he?"

"Your rat?" said Mrs. Resnick. "No, sorry. I think we're going to have to accept that he's made an escape."

I looked around the room. He could have gotten out under the door, or through the heating ducts, or even in someone's backpack. "I guess you're

right," I said. "Do you think he'll be okay?"

Mrs. Resnick nodded as if she was sure of it. "Oh, yes. Rats are very smart. Very adaptable. He's probably happily setting up a new home somewhere in the building."

"What about our project?"

"I know you and Waylon put a lot of work into your training. And I remember you wrote an excellent report. But we'll have to find something else for you to do now. I'll think about it and have an answer for you on Friday."

When I got home, I found my mother lying on the floor in the living room, with my brother lying next to her.

"I'm doing my pregnant-lady exercises," she told me. "Your brother is keeping me company."

I dropped my backpack onto a chair and got

down beside them. "I remember this," I said. "From when you were having Potato. I used to lie down with you and talk to him inside your stomach."

I showed my brother what I meant, and he got the idea right away. He put his mouth on our mother's shirt and yelled for the baby to come out and play.

My mother laughed. "It's a little early for that," she explained. Then she sat up. "Would you like to see a picture of what the baby looks like right now?"

I said nope, but she reached over to the coffee table and picked up a booklet anyway. She thumbed through a couple of pages and then held it out. "Your brother or sister is about five inches long," she said.

My brother looked at the picture and then threw his head back and laughed as if she had just told

him the funniest joke in the world.

I took the booklet for a closer look. It showed a little pink thing, part human, part fish, part . . . "It looks like Eighteen," I said. "It looks like a little rat now. Except Eighteen is cute."

I looked at the picture again. It wasn't a rat. It was a real baby. And that gave me the most astoundishing idea I had ever had in my life. "Hey,

Mom. This booklet sure is science-y, right?"

"Science-y? Well, I guess . . ."

"Mom, when can you have this baby? Like in two weeks? Then you could be my science project!"

My mom laughed really hard. "Oh, no, Clementine. Babies take a long time to grow, and they pick their timing. This baby will be here sometime in early July, but it will keep its birthday a big surprise."

I sighed. What I had said yesterday was right. This baby sure wasn't going to help with any of my problems.

# CHAPTER
## 6

On the bus Wednesday morning, Margaret said I looked even worse. "Completely washed out. Even your teeth have faded. I guess this means you couldn't talk them out of it."

Sometimes Margaret was N-O-T, *not* helpful.

"You can't talk someone out of having a baby, Margaret," I said. "They've already started. It's already kicking my mom and stuff."

"Well, then, what are they going to name it? A fruit, like you, or a vegetable, like your brother?"

I looked at Margaret. That was a really good question. "My brother has a regular name," I reminded her. "I just call him vegetable names to make things fair. Still, I think the baby should have a food name. . . ."

"Maybe a soup name," Margaret said. "Or a sandwich. Or a dessert."

"Those are good ideas, Margaret," I said. Then I rolled up my sleeve and wrote them down on my arm so I wouldn't forget. Not dessert, though—I like dessert. "I know—we should name the baby Mushroom Soup."

"You hate mushroom soup the worst," Margaret said.

"Exactly right."

In school, at Morning Circle Time, Mr. D'Matz said, "I would like to start by sharing something about myself."

All the kids whipped to attention, surprised. Except me. I gave him a tiny secret smile.

"I'm going to be a father soon," he said. "My wife and I are expecting a baby."

Everyone went crazy then, talking at once and making noises like this was the most exciting thing that had ever happened in the history of the world.

Finally Mr. D'Matz held up his hand to calm things down. "I'm wondering how many of you have had new babies come into your families."

About half the kids' hands shot up. I raised my hand, too, but I looked at Mr. D'Matz hard, to remind him about our privacy agreement. He gave me the slightest nod.

"Would anyone like to share what it was like to have a new brother or sister?" he asked the class.

One after the other, kids raised their hands and talked about how great it was to have a new baby come into the family. How cute the babies were, how much fun.

I said my times tables really loud in my head.

"Is there anyone else here who'd like to share something?" Mr. D'Matz looked around the circle. His eyes stopped at me for just a second, and he raised his eyebrows.

"Nope," I said. "Nobody else has anything to share."

The rest of the day didn't get any better. I went to the Lost and Found, and there were eleven winter hats there. None of them was mine. On the way back, I stopped Mr. Riley, the custodian, and asked him to keep an eye out for Eighteen. But he said a sixth grader had knocked a water fountain off the wall, and it would be a miracle if he could keep the whole second floor from flooding. And at lunch, Waylon told me his new plan of using his X-ray vision as a science project, but when he tried to guess what was in my lunch bag, he couldn't even see the juice box poking out of the top.

Back in the classroom, I started worrying about Eighteen again. Danger was everywhere: what if he crawled into a pencil sharpener? I scratched at my elbows. What if he got trapped in a locker? I scraped my itchy shoulders up and down the back of my chair. What if he wandered into the boys' room and got flushed down the drain? My scratchy skin wanted to peel itself off my bones.

Finally I excused myself and left to see Principal Rice.

Okay, fine, I didn't actually excuse myself and leave. My teacher sent me. But I *would* have excused myself and left if I'd had to sit still in my worried skin for one second more.

"It's been a while, Clementine," Mrs. Rice said. "What are we here for today?"

"I'm worried about Eighteen," I said, handing her the note from Mr. D'Matz. "It's making me itchy."

"That's odd," Mrs. Rice said, reading the note. "According to this, we're here to talk about your not distracting the other students."

"You probably just read the note too fast," I said. I added an understanding smile, because I read things too fast sometimes also. "It probably says the other students were distracting *me*. From worrying about Eighteen."

Mrs. Rice read the note again, shook her head, then put it down. "Well, anyway," she said. "You're worried about a number?"

"Oh, no. Eighteen's his name. Our rat. Waylon and I—"

"Oh, right," Mrs. Rice interrupted me. "The one who made the breakout from the science room over the weekend."

"That's him," I said. "This is a really dangerous place if you're a rat. We have to shut down the school and search . . . Wait! You already knew about Eighteen?"

Mrs. Rice nodded. "Mrs. Resnick told me yesterday. I sent a memo to the custodians and the lunchroom staff."

"You already did? Well, good," I said. But somehow I didn't feel good. Finally it hit me. "You mean the custodians knew? Even Mr. Riley?"

Mrs. Rice nodded again. "So everyone's on the lookout. I hope that's going to cut down on the distractions in your classroom, whoever is distracting whom."

I sat there, thinking about all the things that

grown-ups knew and hadn't told kids. And trying to think of a single thing that kids knew and hadn't told grown-ups.

Finally I came up with one. "My teacher is getting a baby. He told us today."

"Yes, I know. It's exciting news, isn't it?"

"You knew that, too?"

"I knew that, too," Mrs. Rice said.

"Can I be all done being here?" I asked.

"That depends," Mrs. Rice said. "Are you still feeling itchy?"

I said no, which was true—now I was feeling too mad to be itchy—and I went back to my classroom.

I was still mad when I got home from school. I announced my bad mood when I opened the door.

"It's just me, Sport," my dad called, coming into the hall. "Your mom's at the library with your brother. What's the problem?"

"Everything," I growled.

My dad pulled his apartment manager keys out of his pocket. "Do you need to take a few rides?"

Usually when I'm upset, riding the service elevator calms me down. Not today.

I shook my head. "What I need is to find my last year's winter hat." I opened the hall closet and dragged out everything that was in the way of the stroller. I climbed up on it to take a look around.

"Careful, there," my dad said. "We're going to need that."

"No we don't," I said. "String Bean walks great now."

"He's still a little guy," my dad pointed out. "His legs still get tired."

I climbed down. "What about my tired legs?" I asked. "I have tired legs all the time. How come nobody cares about them? If I have to walk, he should have to walk."

My dad just looked at me, which made me know I was being too crabby. Still.

"Besides, pretty soon we'll need it for the new baby. Hey, is this what you're looking for?" He handed me my last-year's hat.

It had only three colors. There were no yarn tails sticking out. It looked tight and itchy. I threw it into the back of the closet.

"Want to tell me what else is wrong?" my dad asked.

And suddenly, I *did* have tired legs. I slumped down to the floor in the middle of the closet mess.

My dad sat down beside me. He tucked his keys

back into his pocket, and a pack of gum fell out. "Huh," he said, as if it was a big surprise to him. "Wonder how that got in there." He unwrapped two sticks and gave me one.

We sat there for a few minutes, chomping hard.

"Everything's changing," I said after a while. "Cabbage is tall now. He's having a talking spurt. Margaret is a makeup fiend, and she's trying to move to California. We're  going to be five and not four anymore, but we're out of rooms. And I'm stuck with Waylon for a partner in science."

"You're right," my dad said. "Things are changing. We can't help that. It's life.

But I'm confused about Waylon. Didn't you tell me last week you felt lucky that you'd gotten him for a partner?"

"That was last week. Before I found out."

"Before you found out what?"

"That he wants to walk through a wall."

"Excuse me?"

"Exactly," I said.

I chewed my gum for a while, then I explained the whole situation to him.

"And you don't believe in superpowers," my dad said when I finished.

I looked at him. "Well . . . I don't know about that. But I don't believe Waylon has any."

"That's a tough one," said my dad. "You don't think there's a science project there, but you don't want to hurt his feelings. I wish I could think of something to help."

I leaned up against my dad and we chewed our

gum for a while, until I realized I felt better. That is the miracle about gum. "Hey, Dad," I said, side-smiling at him. "You know what might help? If I could wear your tool belt . . ."

My dad side-smiled back. "Oh, too bad. It's in the vault. I have to keep it locked up because it's so special. That tool belt was given to me by the President of the United States in appreciation for my lifelong service to this country."

"Dad."

"Seriously. It was in the Oval Office. I wore a tux."

"Dad. It was in Hardware Depot. Aisle seven. You wore your raggedy green pants."

"Oh right," my dad said. "I can't believe your mother let me wear those pants out of the house."

"So where is it, really?"

"Really? Well, really, your Uncle Frank was

here this morning. He's putting up some shelves in his kitchen, and I let him borrow it."

I jumped up and spit my gum out onto the back of my hand. "Dad! You let Uncle Frank borrow it? But you never even let me touch it!"

My dad got up, too. "Clementine, what is the deal with my tool belt? I've never seen you so obsessed."

"It's just . . . it's just . . ." I said, trying to figure it out myself. "It looks so cool and it's got all your tools, and if I wore it, I could build something anytime I wanted."

"And you want to build something?"

"Yes! Of course!"

My dad looked at me like he was seeing a new person. "I didn't know that about you," he said at last.

"Well, I didn't know it, either," I admitted. "Until I saw that tool belt."

Thursday, all anyone could talk about at school was how great it was to have a new kid come into your family, as if babies were just cute pets, or really fun toys. The only person who wasn't talking about that was Waylon. Instead, he talked about his new idea for our science project, which was to use his brain waves to cook food.

Margaret was waiting for me on the bus home with a pot of orange cheek-glitter. When I threw up my arms to protect my cheeks, my backpack fell off and my IMPORTANT PAPERS folder flew out.

I had to crawl under the seats to get all my papers back, and then I spent the whole ride trying to wipe the melted slush-mud off them.

By the time I got to my apartment, let me tell you my mood was B-A-D, *bad* again. It was hard to keep it that way, though.

Moisturizer was waiting at the door, and he jumped into my arms and started to lick my face. A little of the blueberry pancake smell from breakfast was still in the air, mixed up with the smell from the pine branches my mom had brought in to decorate with. Mrs. Watson upstairs was practicing her harp, which makes it sound like we have angels for neighbors.

I felt my bad mood starting to melt. "I'm home!" I called.

My dad came out and put his finger to his lips and pointed into the living room, where my brother and my mom were conked out on the couch having a nap together. They were covered in trucks and

books, and they looked so cute, I wanted to draw a picture of them.

"Growing a baby is a lot of work," my dad whispered. "Your mom's going to be a little tired these days."

He motioned to the kitchen. "I'm about to make some of my secret-recipe toast. You hungry?"

I said yes even though his secret recipe is just "Put bread in the toaster," because I was starving.

When the toast popped up, we carried it to the table and spread it with almond butter, which is like peanut butter except it doesn't make my little brother's head explode from being allergic.

I spread grape jelly over the almond butter and took a big bite. "See, Dad?" I said. "How nice our family is this way, two and two? Two in the living room and two in the kitchen."

Dad reached over and opened the marmalade, which is a kind of jelly that grown-ups pretend to like even though it has orange grinds in it, which we throw away for a reason. He spread it over his toast, all the way to the edge the way I taught him, then he took a big bite, too. "Yep," he said after a while. "Four's a good number. Five's a good number, too."

"Two asleep and two awake," I said. I spread a little extra jelly on a spot I had missed. "Four's a perfect number."

My dad took another bite of toast. Then he surprised me. "Clementine, how old are you?" he asked.

"You know. Eight and a half."

"No, I mean exactly," he said. "How old are you exactly?"

"Down to the hours and minutes?"

"Just the days." He took another bite of toast.

"Three thousand one hundred and fourteen."

My father looked up and stared at me. He dropped his toast. Then he wiped his mouth with his napkin and stood, shaking his head. "I can't believe I almost missed this. Finish up and get your coat on, Sport."

My dad wouldn't tell me where we were going, just left a note for my mom and started driving.

To Hardware Depot. Like on Sunday. He went right to aisle seven again.

"Dad! Did Uncle Frank lose your new tool belt?"

"No. He returned it this morning."

"Well, then, did *you* lose it?"

Most of me wanted the answer to be no, because it was so special to him. But a little teeny-tiny part of me wanted him to say yes. *Yes, Clementine, I lost something important. . . . It happens to people all the time. No big deal*, he'd say. *So you shouldn't get upset when it happens to you. Like if you lose a special hat, for instance.*

But he didn't say any of that. "Clementine," he said instead, "in my family, a person's three thousand one hundred and fifteenth day is a very special day. It's the day when—"

"Three thousand one hundred and fourteenth day," I corrected him.

"Oh, right. You look older than that today. It

got me confused." He winked. "Anyway, it's the day when the people in my family get their first tool belts." He spread his hands out over the display. "Which one would you like?"

There were so many to choose from, which meant so many to not-choose, which I hate. A lot were brown and leathery, like my dad's, but they were different brownnesses, and different leatherinesses. And some other kinds were black and some were red, and some had Velcro fasteners and some had regular belt buckles. They were all beautiful. I picked up one that was butterscotch pudding–colored with silver hooks, like my dad's, and started to wrap it around my waist.

"May I help you?"

In Hardware Depot the salespeople wear yellow aprons with name tags on them. The one who had snuck up on us was named Chuck.

"My partner and I are getting a tool belt today," my dad said. He put his arm around my shoulders.

Salesman Chuck bent his head way over, as if it was a really long way down to look at such a little kid, and then he looked up at my dad and winked. "I think I have just the thing for you folks," he said. "Follow me."

There was something about the way he winked at my father that I didn't like—like he was sharing some kind of grown-ups-only joke with him—but I dropped the belt and we followed him anyway.

And you will not believe where he took us!

I crossed my arms over my chest and waited for my dad to explain to Salesman Chuck that it was my three thousand one hundred and fourteenth day, which meant I got a *real* tool belt, not a pretend one from the "Li'l Carpenter" section, thank you very much!

But my father just said the "Thank you very much" part, and then he picked out a little blue plastic tool belt and dropped it into our cart!

"But—but—but . . ." I started. And then I couldn't talk anymore because I was too confused from feeling crashed down and furious all at once. And besides, if my dad didn't know he'd just ruined the whole day—maybe even my whole life—I was never going to speak to him again.

He touched my shoulder and pointed to the dumb blue tool belt. "This ought to keep your brother happy," he said. Then he turned to the salesman. "We're going to head back to aisle seven now," he told him. "My partner needs a *real* tool belt."

And then we left Salesman Chuck, who wasn't winking anymore, and went back to aisle seven. This time I didn't have any problem not-choosing—I picked the one that looked the most like my dad's, wrapped it around my waist twice, and buckled it. "Let's go," I said.

"Not yet, Sport." My dad picked out a wide blue wristband and fastened it around my wrist. It was heavier than it looked. "It's magnetized," he explained. "For holding the nails and small tools you need for the job."

And we still weren't finished! "Not much sense

owning a tool belt if you haven't got any tools to keep in it," Dad said.

We marched over to the tools section, and I picked out a tool for every holder on the belt: a hammer, a screwdriver, a wrench, two kinds of pliers, a chisel, a tape measure, and a little level. My dad showed me how to hold each one the proper way, so I could see which one felt right in my hand. I didn't pick the biggest ones, but they weren't little either. They were just right.

I filled that tool belt, which was all M-I-N-E, *mine* now, with tools that were all mine now, too. When I turned around they felt big and bumpy and heavy, but good. And then we clunked over to the cash register and paid for everything and said good-bye, which felt good, too.

My dad started up the car, and we pulled out of the parking lot.

I reached over the seat and tilted the visor down until I could see my new tool belt in the mirror. My dad was right—I did look older than three thousand one hundred and fourteen days.

"The baby can't touch this tool belt," I said.

"Absolutely not," my dad agreed.

"And not Carrot, either," I went on.

"No, not your brother either," Dad said. "He'll have to be satisfied with the one we bought him."

"It's just for me."

"It's just for you."

"Because I'm the oldest."

"Right. Because you're old enough for the responsibility. The responsibility of wearing an heirloom from the Ming dynasty—"

"Dad! Don't wreck this!"

"Okay, sorry. Really."

I put my hand on the hammer and squeezed hard. "I'm sorry, too," I said.

"For what?" Dad asked.

"For saying it's unfair about the baby. He's just a baby—he doesn't mean to be unfair."

My dad was quiet for a minute. Then he pulled

the car over and turned the key off, which meant Here Comes a Serious Talk. He turned around to look at me.

"Clementine, I've been thinking," he said. "I tried to put myself in your place, and I asked myself, What if my kids told me they were getting another dad? That they loved me just fine but they thought our family had room for another father, and they hadn't asked for my opinion. How would I feel about that, I asked myself. And the answer was that I would feel a lot like you seem to feel."

"But that's not the same thing at all," I told him.

"Well, not exactly, no. It's different with parents, of course. But the point is, it helped me understand how you felt. I just want you to know that I get it."

# CHAPTER
## 8

When we got home, my mom was in the kitchen making dinner. I started to give her a big hug, but then I realized something: I was hugging the new baby, too. I stepped back and hugged her on the side. Then I gave her belly a really small pat.

"How's Mushroom Soup doing today?" I asked.

"Mushroom soup?" my mom asked. "I'm starting a casserole here. No mushrooms at all."

"No, I mean the baby. The baby has to have a food name," I explained. "You like soup. How about a soup name? Like Mushroom Soup—how about that?"

My mother laughed. "We haven't thought about names yet," she said. "But when we do, I doubt Mushroom Soup will be a top contender." Then she looked down and saw what I was wearing.

"Bill, this isn't safe!" she said, turning me around. "She's going to trip over these tools. Plus, they're mauling her. That wrench is going to crack her little shinbone. . . ."

My dad stood up for me. "The people in my family are known for their extra-hard shinbones. We all develop extraordinary strength and balance from wearing tool belts as children. So it's actually a plus."

I could see my mom was getting ready for a big argument, so I thought it was smart to get out of there while my dad was ahead. "I'm going to go visit Margaret for a minute," I said. And then I ran out.

I clunked into the elevator and used my wrench

to press the floor number five button. I rang the
bell with the screwdriver. Mitchell opened the
door, and his eyes nearly popped out when he saw
what I was wearing. "Dude-ette!" he cried. He
gave me a high five. "Awesome!"

Mitchell calls me great names like Dude-ette

because he wants to be my boyfriend. So far, I haven't let him be my boyfriend, because I don't want one. But if I ever do want one, which I won't, and if it's ever Mitchell, which it won't be, now I knew what I should wear on our first date: my tool belt!

"Hey, Mitchell," I said. "What was your science fair project when you were in third grade?"

Mitchell squinted and scratched his head. "Third grade is ancient history. Oh, I remember! Worms. I grew worms, measured how they made the soil better or something."

"Was that a good project?"

"Good? Are you kidding? It was *awesome*. Margaret didn't come in my room for a whole month!"

"No, I meant . . . oh, never mind. I don't have a month to grow worms. I need an instant, just-add-water kind of project."

"How come?"

I explained the whole Waylon problem.

Mitchell shook his head sadly when I was done. "Dude's going to pay," he said.

"What do you mean?" I asked.

"That kid gets up in front of everybody, says he can walk through a wall and then doesn't do it?" He shuddered and made the baseball "You're out!" sign. "Dude's toast. Burnt toast."

I hadn't thought about that.

Margaret came into the hall just then. "What's the matter with you? Why are you looking so worried?" she asked me. Then she saw my tool belt. "Did you break your back? Is that a brace?" She leaned in for a closer look. "Oh, for goodness' sakes," she muttered. "You are crazy."

"I'm not crazy, Margaret!" I said, following her down the hall to her room. "Now I can build things. Maybe I'll be a builder when I grow up. That's not crazier than you being a makeup artist."

Margaret turned around then, with a dreamy expression on her face from the magic words *you being a makeup artist.*

"I might not even have to wait until I grow up," she said. "When my father finds out how good I'm getting, he'll probably let me start working in his studio right away."

"You're not going to California, Margaret," I reminded her. "Because your mother's not having a baby. Besides, even if she did, maybe you'd like it. Lots of kids like having new babies in their families."

Margaret looked at me like I was out of my mind. "If I were you I would be moving out right now. I would be on the next plane to California. With my makeup bag . . . Hey!" Margaret snapped her fingers. "I should practice now, on you!"

"No way," I said. "I'm never going to wear makeup."

"You'll have to someday. If you want people to like you, you have to wear makeup."

"That's not true."

"Yes, it is. Especially if you're going to go around wearing a tool belt."

"There's no rule about that!" I cried. "My mother doesn't wear makeup, and lots of people like her."

Margaret shrugged. "Your mother is pregnant," she reminded me.

Which I knew.

Margaret looked into her mirror and flipped her hair. Her face melted into a dreamy smile again. "And another thing—in California, I could have a new hairdo anytime I want. There are hairdoers who practically live at my father's commercial-making studio."

Suddenly I couldn't stand to hear one more word about Margaret going to California. "Okay, fine," I said. "You can put makeup on me." This is called Throwing Someone Off the Track.

I guess Margaret was afraid I was going to change my mind, because she shoved me into the seat at her dressing table and slapped a towel around my shoulders before I could say another word. She shut the door and rubbed her hands together. Then she pulled a big pink case out from her closet.

Her cat, Mascara, went electric and ducked under the bed when he saw that case, so I figure she had been practicing on him, too. Inside the case were dozens of brushes and sponges and tubes and little jars.

Margaret examined them for a while and finally selected a glittery tube. "We'll start with a base of Sun-kissed Peach," she said. "I'll apply it double-thick, to try to hide those freckles."

"I like my freckles!" I said. "Don't hide them!"

Too late. Margaret was already dabbing gunk on my face and rubbing it in, and dabbing more gunk on and smearing it around some more. Every once in a while she'd step back and hold her thumb up and squint at me, like a cartoon artist. Then she'd nod as if she was doing an excellent job.

Every time I wanted to jump off the chair and go home, I remembered about Margaret leaving to go live in California. Margaret is my friend. Even though she is kind of a bossy girl, and even though sometimes she can get kind of crazy about her rules, and even though I sometimes don't recognize her anymore, she is my friend. And I figured that maybe if my friend could paint makeup all over my face and pretend she was an artist, she wouldn't move away to California.

Suddenly Margaret screamed. She clapped her

hand over my mouth to shush me, even though she was the one who'd screamed, and even though now she was going to have to wash that hand a hundred times because she is a germ-maniac.

"What's the matter?" I hissed through her hand.

Margaret had turned white and her eyes were popping out. "My mother and Alan are back!" she whispered.

"So what?" I asked.

She jumped out into the hall, spun around, and jumped back in again. Margaret takes all kinds of dance lessons—I could see that they were really paying off.

"We have to go to your apartment," she said. She tugged my arms out of my sweatshirt sleeves, pulled the sweatshirt up over my head, and then tied the sleeves over it. "We can go out now," she told me.

"I can't see!"

I heard Margaret growl, and then she unzipped the zipper a little and tugged the opening over one of my eyes and shoved me out the door. She pushed me into the hall past the kitchen.

"Is that a Clementine under there?" I heard Alan say. "Or maybe an apple or a plum or a banana?"

Margaret's mother laughed as if Alan had made

a really funny joke. Which he had not. "Your mother told me the news today," she called out. "A new baby—how exciting!"

"Nope, not exciting!" I said through my sweatshirt. "I mean, it wouldn't be exciting for *your* family to have another baby. You have just the right number of kids right now!"

I was going to say more, like that her kid might move away if she had another baby, but then Margaret gave me an extra-hard push toward the front door.

"We're going down to Clementine's now," she called back to her mother. "So, bye."

Down in my apartment, we got into my room without anyone seeing us. "How come you want to keep it a secret about the makeup, Margaret?" I asked.

"The makeup's not secret," Margaret said. "It's just that my mother gets into a bad mood whenever something reminds her of Heather. She won't even say her name—just calls her Number Five." Margaret opened her case up again and pulled out some more paint. "Turn your face up. It's time to do your eyes."

Finally Margaret said I was finished and let me look in the mirror. Let me tell you, it was a good thing I'd seen that horror movie with my Uncle Frank, because otherwise I would have fainted from being so scared.

"Aaauuurrrggghhh!" I yelled. "I look like a brain-sucking alien vampire swamp creature!"

Margaret stepped back and studied me. "You kind of do," she admitted. Her shoulders got saggy.

"That's okay, Margaret. Maybe you could be that kind of makeup artist. Maybe you could make actors look scary."

Margaret brightened up. "Special effects!"

"Right! Except . . ." I sighed. "Except I don't want you to move to California."

Margaret helped me wash the makeup off. Then we looked at our bare faces in the mirror for a while.

"I wouldn't really move," she said. "I just like to think about it when things drive me crazy."

"Oh," I said. "Well, good."

# CHAPTER
## 9

After dinner, my grandmother called and asked to talk to me. "I got your letter. Don't you worry for another minute," she said. "I've already started you a new hat."

"But will it have all my favorite colors in it again? Will it be soft, and fit like your hands?"

"I'll do my best," my grandmother promised. "Now, the other reason I called is that I realized I never finished that story I was telling. Put me on speakerphone so everyone can hear, would you, darling?"

I said sure, and then she started over again. "Now, that time with the boys and the garden hose—oh, that was a good one. Your father was supposed to be in his room, because—"

My father jumped up from the couch and grabbed the phone and turned off the speakerphone. "Well, we have to go now, Mom," he said. "It's a school night. Kids have to get to bed. Bye." Then he hung up.

He told my mom to go put her feet up on the couch and sent me to get in my pajamas. My father is pretty good at the Throwing-Someone-Off-the-Track trick. But since I invented it, it doesn't work on me.

I raced into my pajamas in five seconds flat. "So what happened with the garden hose?" I asked, skidding back into the living room. "Did you squirt Uncle Frank? Was it summertime?"

"Your father's finishing up the dishes," Mom said from the couch. "I'd like to hear the end of that story, too, so why don't you— Hey! What in . . ." Then she jumped up from the couch more suddenly than I think people should do when they are growing other actual people inside them, and yanked up my pajama legs.

"What happened to you?" she cried. "You look like you were run over by a train!"

I looked. From the knees down, I did look like I'd been run over by a train! "Can I wear shorts to school tomorrow?" I asked, turning my legs around so I could admire the bruises, which were even better than the ones I'd gotten jumping from the bleachers at Mitchell's ball game last year.

"Clementine, what happened to you?" my mother cried again. "Did you have a fall? Did you . . . Oh. Oh, for heaven's sake." She clapped her hand to her forehead. "Bill," she called. When my dad poked his head out from the kitchen, she pointed to my legs with an I-told-you-so look.

"Oh," my dad said, coming over to take a closer look. "Battle wounds from the tools. Sorry. Does it hurt, Sport?"

"No! It feels great! Can I wear shorts tomorrow?"

"Absolutely not," my mother said. "It's the middle of winter. And people would think . . . well,

I don't know what they'd think, but it wouldn't be good. And the other thing you can't wear is that tool belt anymore."

"Mom, no!" I cried.

My mother folded her arms across her chest.

"But I got this tool belt at the White House," I tried. "The president gave it to me for lifelong service to my country. In the Oval Office!"

My mom just shook her head.

"It's an heirloom from the Ming dynasty!"

My mom rolled her eyes and sighed.

I looked over at my dad to see if he could help, but he just raised his palms, as if to say, What can I do?

Then I had a better idea. "I'll wear my winter boots. The tall ones with the padding."

My mom started to say no, but then I could see she was giving up, like maybe she was too tired to argue about things anymore. This might be a good side to having a pregnant mother.

"Fine," she said. "You can wear the tool belt if you wear your winter boots underneath. That's the rule."

I jumped up and hugged her before she could change her mind.

# CHAPTER

## I O

When I came out for breakfast Friday morning, my mom grabbed my shoulders and turned me around. "Go right back into your room to take that off," she said. "You are not wearing that tool belt to school."

"But I'm going to put my winter boots on!"

"Not to school," my mother said in her That's-final voice.

"But you said!" I tried in my I'm-a-kid-so-I've-got-plenty-of-energy-to-outlast-you voice.

"Not to school," my mother said back in her

I-am-not-kidding-and-I've-got-plenty-of-energy-too voice. I guess it's not *that* tiring to be growing a baby.

My father looked up from pouring coffee and pointed to my bedroom.

So I went back to my room and took off my tool belt and hung it up over my bedpost. I rolled my sleeve down over the magnetized wristband so it wouldn't show. Nobody had made any rules about that wristband yet, and I had big plans for it today.

At recess, I gathered all the kids around me. "I woke up with a superpower," I announced. "It's from hanging around with Waylon lately. You can call me Magneto-Girl!"

Then I scattered the nails I'd brought from my dad's workbench in a pile on the asphalt. "Stick to me!" I ordered the nails.

I swept my arm over the piles of nails, and they all clattered up through the air and clinked onto my wrist.

The kids went wild. But I wasn't done. I went over to the swings and held my arm out to one of the chains.

"Come to me," I ordered the swing.

And it did! The swing clinked to my wrist and held fast as I raised my arm and swooshed it around.

The kids went totally crazy then, climbing all over me, trying to grab my arm.

Waylon held them back. "Leave her alone," he said. "That's the way it is with superpowers. She doesn't have to tell about it if she doesn't want to."

Waylon stayed with me all through recess, to make sure nobody bothered me. When we lined up, I thanked him. "It's just a magnetic wristband," I whispered. "For carpenters to hold nails and stuff."

"I know," Waylon said. "My aunt has one."

"Oh. Well, that means I don't really have any superpowers, you know."

"That's okay," Waylon said. "I had to pretend in the beginning, too."

I tried again. "Waylon, I've been thinking. I don't think our project should be about your superpowers."

"But they're really great," Waylon said. "And really science-y."

"I know," I said. "But Superman never used his for a science project. None of the superheroes I've ever heard of did. They all saved their powers for fighting evil. That's what I think you should do."

Waylon looked like he was thinking about my idea, but before he could tell me what he decided, the bell rang. Right away, we lined up for science.

When we got there, I realized the science room

was a dangerous place for someone wearing a magnetic wristband. Cages and microscopes and training bells and dozens of other metal things were just waiting to get me into trouble.

I unpeeled the Velcro and tossed my wristband onto the bookshelf. It skittered over the top and fell down behind.

Things disappeared down there, and I couldn't afford to lose anything else. "Will you help me move the bookshelf?" I asked Waylon.

We slid the bookshelf out, and there was my wristband, all right, stuck to a metal heating-vent grate halfway up the wall. I reached for it and tugged. The grate swung up a little way before the wristband let go.

I bent down. There was something inside the duct. Something soft. Something fluffy. Something made of all my favorite colors.

"My hat!" I cried. "My hat's inside the heating

duct!" I tugged up on the loose grate and it came right off in my hands. Then I reached in for my hat, so happy!

And just in time I saw. It wasn't my hat. It was a wad of shredded yarn bits that used to be my hat. I looked closer. "Waylon, look!" I whispered. "Eighteen! I found Eighteen, too!"

Sure enough, curled up all cozy inside the wool that used to be my hat, peeking over the rim, was Eighteen. Very carefully, I slid the hat-nest onto

the palm of my hand and pulled it out.

And got the surprise of my life.

Tucked into the furry curl that was Eighteen
were five *un*-furry little
curls, pink as erasers.
They were squirming
around and peeking
through their mother's
fur as if they were pretty

excited about getting out of that boring heating
duct.

"Babies! Eighteen had babies!" Waylon cried.

Which was a big mistake, because all the kids
came stampeding over. The babies started to
shiver and burrow into their mother's fur.

"Be careful, be careful! Stay back!" I told
everyone, but in a whisper so I didn't scare the rat
babies any more than they already were. "They're
just little. You have to stay back and be quiet! I'm

going to put them in a cage now, so they can have some peace."

Mrs. Resnick opened up Eighteen's old cage, but I reminded her about the hole. She got another one, and I filled it with nice soft clean wood shavings and gently slid the hat-nest in. "We have to put it in a dark corner now," I said. "It's too bright for them in here."

Waylon came over and helped me move the cage. "I guess we can go back to our old project now," he said. He sounded kind of happy about that, as though it was a relief.

"Can we?" I asked Mrs. Resnick.

Mrs. Resnick said she didn't see any problem at all putting Eighteen back in training on Monday. "Just make sure you write it into your notes that she took a week off. We'll call it a maternity leave."

Waylon and I made a new sign for the cage with everybody's names: Eighteen, Eighteen and

One Fifth, Eighteen and Two Fifths, Eighteen and Three Fifths, Eighteen and Four Fifths, Eighteen and Five Fifths. Then I stood guard over the cage for the rest of the period to make sure the babies were all right.

Back in Mr. D'Matz's class that afternoon, I had to hear a lot of "Clementine-pay-attention!"s. And just like before, I *was* paying attention: I was paying attention to all the things Eighteen's new family might need over the weekend.

When the two-fifteen bell rang, I ran back to the science room. "I'm going to take the cage home tonight," I told Mrs. Resnick. "They might get hungry or lonely, and they might need something."

"Well, I don't know . . ." Mrs. Resnick said.

"I will take good care of them," I told her. "I was very protective of my little brother when he was born. Also, I showed good sense. Immensely good sense."

"Well, after watching you this afternoon, I have no trouble believing that," Mrs. Resnick said. "So yes, that sounds like a good plan."

I wrapped the cage up in my coat and carried it carefully to the bus, and on the ride home I didn't let anyone bother those little babies.

When I got home, I brought the cage right over to my mom. "See! That's why Eighteen was getting fatter! He was a she, and she was growing babies inside her. Just like you."

"Well, let's hope there's only *one* baby in here!" She lifted her shirt and patted her stomach.

"Hey, you *are* fatter!" I said.

My mom rubbed her belly. "Yep, a little. It's starting to show."

"What does it feel like?" I asked. "To have a whole new person growing inside you?"

My mom sat down on the couch and leaned back and thought for a while. A pretty smile spread over her face. "That's a big question," she said slowly. "A big answer. But I'll try. It feels like . . . it feels like you have the most wonderful secret that makes everything . . . Oh, I know! Remember what you said when you got your kitten? You said that afterward, it sounded like all the regular noise in the world had turned into music. Well, that's what it's like, Clementine. The wonderful secret of having a baby coming makes all the world's noise turn into music."

"Did you feel that way when you were going to have me, too?" I asked.

"Oh, honey," my mom said, putting her arm around me. "I *still* feel like that with you."

I gave her a big hug, and this time, I didn't care at all that I was hugging the baby, too. Then I got up and brought the cage into my room, where Eighteen's family would be safe. I pulled out a sheet of paper and wrote another letter to my grandmother, so she would know that her hat was still making someone happy and warm.

Then I took out the notebook where I keep reminders to myself for when I'm a grown-up.

After TATTOOS—YES! I had written: BABIES—NO.

I crossed off NO and wrote, WELL, MAYBE.

And then I went into the kitchen—I had one more important thing to do.

After I did it, I sat down and waited. The first person to come in was my father. He went to the refrigerator and took out some grapes. "Hey," he said. "The FAMILY MEETING! sign is up again. Who called the meeting?"

I gave a shrug. "The meeting's tonight," I said. "I guess we'll find out then."

"I see," said my dad. He popped a few grapes into his mouth and gave me a funny look.

My mother came in next and noticed right away. She looked at my dad and he shook his head. She looked at me. "What's on the agenda?" she asked.

I shrugged again. "The meeting's tonight. I guess you'll have to wait until then to find out."

My mom laughed. "Well, fair's fair. All right, I'll wait."

\* \* \*

Finally it was after dinner. "I called this meeting," I said when we were all in our places, "to talk about something important. Our family is having a baby. And we need to protect it, to keep it safe.

"We need to make some rules. Like, we have to tell Gram and Pop, 'No golf carts or bingo in Florida.' And when George the plumber comes, we have to check his bag to make sure the baby didn't crawl inside. And Uncle Frank can't take the baby to the movies. And what if it's allergic to something, like Yam is? Also, we'd better get Margaret to teach us about germ protection, and Mom, you should put a lock on the art-supply organizer I got you."

I turned my brother around on my lap. "And you, Spinach," I said, "you can't put your trucks in the baby's food. And I'll keep my door shut,

because Dad, what if you're right about the Black Hole under my bed? What if things really do get lost forever there? How are we going to keep the baby safe—"

"Hold on, Sport, hold on," my dad said. "We've

got lots of time. The baby won't really be motoring around and getting into anything for a good long time."

"But, Dad, we've got to—"

"Your father's right," my mom said. "We've got a couple of years before we have to worry about all those things. Why, by the time the baby is walking, you'll be ten. That's plenty of time to get ready. But I'm glad to see what a good sister you're going to be."

All the rest of the things I had ready to say fell out of my head. "What did you just say? I'll be ten?"

"That's right," my mom said. "By the time the baby is in any danger of walking into your room, you'll be ten years old."

"I'll be ten?" I repeated. "Ten years old? Like Margaret?"

My parents nodded.

"I'll be ten," I said. I sat back to try to imagine that. "I'll be bigger, you know," I said.

"Gigantic," my dad agreed. "We'll probably have to cut a hole in the ceiling. . . ."

"Dad. Seriously. I'll be bigger, you know. And I'll be able to build lots of things."

"Probably," my dad answered. "A lot of things will be different."

Zucchini slid down and ran over to his favorite cupboard and started pulling out the pots and pans.

I thought about how Margaret had changed when she turned ten. "I won't turn into a makeup fiend," I promised everybody. "In fact, I won't change at all. I'll just be me, but bigger."

My parents laughed.

"Oh, you'll change," my mom said. "We'll all stay the same in some ways, but we'll all change, too. You kids most of all."

My dad nodded and spread his hands out to

the clutter of pots and pans my brother had made. "And it will feel crazy sometimes, and like it's moving too fast. But it will be fine, we'll adapt. Because this is how we roll, Clementine. This is how we roll."

# CHAPTER
## I I

When I woke up Saturday morning, I saw it had snowed during the night. Usually I think it is unfair when it snows on the weekend instead of a school day, but today it seemed just right. My brother and I raced through our breakfasts, and raced into our snowsuits, and then raced out to where my dad was shoveling. I took the extra shovel and helped. My brother dove into the drifts and pretended he was a snow bomb.

When the steps and sidewalk were clear, I took Cabbage aside. "Dad's going to turn around in a minute and say, 'Whew, time to head in.' When he does, you go sit on the shovel."

Sure enough, my dad scraped up a few final loads of snow, then looked around at the nice clear steps and said, "Whew, time to head in." I gave Brussels Sprout a little shove and he plopped down on the shovel, and I motioned for him to zip his lips.

Our father trudged around to the back of the building, dragging the shovel behind him muttering, "Hmmm . . . this shovel didn't feel nearly this heavy when I started out. I must be really tired!" just the way he always used to with me. I stood on the street for a minute and watched before following them. I felt split exactly in two: half of the Clementine sections were sorry I was too big to ride on the shovel. And half of them really liked seeing my brother laughing into his

mittens at the great joke he was playing on
our dad.

When our dad gave me a wink as he passed by,
the second half won.

Inside, we peeled off our wet snowsuits. I was just about to go and tell my mom about Cucumber riding the shovel when my dad touched my shoulder.

"Can you spare a minute?"

"Sure," I said. "What's up?"

My dad nodded to the door. "Let's step out into my office."

I followed him into the hall and he closed the door behind us. "What I want to talk about is a secret from your mother."

"Like your green pants?" I asked. "Are you going to wear them out again?"

"No, not like my green pants. This is something good. It's a surprise for when the baby comes. To celebrate."

"What is it?"

"Well, I've been thinking about something you said—about our table being wrong. You remember, because it has four sides, and how it's perfect now because we each have a place but it won't work when there are five of us. I think you're right—that table won't fit our family soon."

"We could get another chair," I said. "We could squeeze two on one side. I guess." I didn't feel great about that solution, but I added a cheerful smile anyway.

My father reached over and scrambled up my hair, which he does when he's extra happy with me. "That's a good plan, Sport," he said. "And that'd be just fine for some families. But I know how to make furniture. And I have a daughter who wants to build something. What I'm thinking is that you and I should build our new family a new table. A round table, a table that all five of us can sit around. What do you think?"

I thought about that for a while, because I knew my dad was seriously asking me for my opinion. "Well," I said finally, "a round table is a good idea. It would be just fine for some families. But you can make furniture. And I want to build something. So how about if you and I build a table that's *exactly* right for our new family: a table with five sides, one for everybody?"

My father stared at me, with a slow smile sliding over his face. He nodded, then nodded some more. "Partner," he said at last, "go get your tool belt."

# Clementine

Clementine is having not so good of a week.
- On Monday she's sent to the principal's office for cutting off Margaret's hair.
- Tuesday, Margaret's mother is mad at her.
- Wednesday, she's sent to the principal . . . again.
- Thursday, Margaret stops speaking to her.
- Friday starts with yucky eggs and gets worse.
- And by Saturday, even her mother is mad at her.

Okay, fine. Clementine is having a DISASTROUS week.

★"Humorous scenarios tumble together, blending picturesque dialogue with a fresh perspective as only the unique Clementine can offer. . . . Frazee's engaging pen-and-ink drawings capture the energy and fresh-faced expressions of the irrepressible heroine. . . . A delightful addition to any beginning chapter-book collection."    —*School Library Journal* (starred review)

- A *Child* magazine Best Book of the Year
- A *Nick Jr.* Best Book of the Year
- A *Publishers Weekly* Best Book of the Year
- A *School Library Journal* Best Book of the Year
- A New York Public Library Book for Reading and Sharing
- A National Parenting Publication Gold Award Winner

# The Talented Clementine

Winner or washout?

When it comes to tackling third grade, Clementine is at the top of her game—okay, so maybe not *all* the time. After her teacher announces that the third and fourth graders will be putting on a talent show, Clementine panics. She doesn't sing or dance or play an instrument. She can't even *hop* with finesse. And as if she didn't feel bad enough, her perfect best friend, Margaret, has so many talents she has to alphabetize them to keep them straight.

As the night of the big "Talent-palooza" draws closer, Clementine is desperate for an act, *any* act. But the unexpected talent she demonstrates at the show surprises everyone—most of all herself.

This *Clementine* sequel is sure to bring the house down!

★ "Clementine is a true original, an empathetic human being with the observant eye of a real artist and a quirky, matter-of-fact way of expressing herself. Frazee's line drawings are plentiful and just right. . . . Early chapter-book readers will jump at the chance to spend another eventful week with Clementine."
—*School Library Journal* (starred review)

# Clementine's Letter

Clementine can't believe her ears—her beloved teacher, Mr. D'Matz, might be leaving them for the rest of the year to go on a research trip to Egypt! No other teacher has ever understood her impulsiveness, her itch to draw constantly, or her need to play Beat the Clock when the day feels too long. And in his place, he's left a substitute with a whole new set of rules that Clementine just can't figure out. The only solution, she decides, is to hatch a plan to get Mr. D'Matz back. If it means ruining her teacher's once-in-a-lifetime chance—well, it'll be worth it. Won't it?

★"Irrepressible and delightful Clementine is back. . . . She shines with a vibrant spirit that can never be completely extinguished, even when she is feeling down. Frazee's pen-and-ink drawings perfectly capture Clementine's personality and her world."

—*School Library Journal* (starred review)

# Clementine,
## Friend of the Week

It's Clementine's turn to be Friend of the Week! She gets to be line leader, collect the lunch money, and feed the fish. Even better, the other kids will make her a booklet, full of the things they value about having her in the class. After reading her friend Margaret's booklet, Clementine begins to get nervous and a little jealous—she *has* to get a great booklet now. Fortunately, she has a lot of astounding ideas for getting the kids to write great stuff about her. Unfortunately, just as she's working on the best one, something terrible happens to her beloved kitten, Moisturizer. Worst of all, exactly when she needs a friend the most, Margaret lets her down.

Or does she . . . ?

★"Pennypacker's writing once again brings creativity, humor, and sensitivity to Clementine and her world. Black-and-white line illustrations grace the book, capturing the child's personality and varied emotions. A must-have. . . . Fans will be in for another fun serving of their favorite girl named after a fruit."
—*School Library Journal* (starred review)